WHAT ABOUT ME?

When Brothers and Sisters Get Sick

by Allan Peterkin, M.D.

illustrated by Frances Middendorf

Magination Press • Washington, DC

For Peter, Elizabeth, Corinne, and all of us who
have lived through illness with a brother or sister

Library of Congress Cataloging-in-Publication Data
Peterkin, Allan.
    What about me? : when brothers and sisters get sick / by Allan
Peterkin ; illustrated by Frances Middendorf.
      p.   cm.
    Summary: Laura experiences conflicting emotions when her brother
becomes seriously ill. Includes suggestions for parents to help
their well children cope with a chronically ill sibling.
    ISBN 0-945354-48-7. — ISBN 0-945354-49-5 (pbk.)
    1. Sick children—Family relationships—Juvenile literature.
2. Brothers and sisters—Juvenile literature. [1. Sick.
2. Brothers and sisters.] I. Middendorf, Frances, ill. II. Title.
RJ47.5.P386 1992
618.92—dc20   92-20035
                                          CIP
                                          AC

Manufactured in the United States of America
10 9 8 7 6 5 4

Introduction for Parents

When children become seriously ill, their brothers and sisters are often confused and experience conflicting emotions. Any illness or hospitalization of a sibling can be traumatic to children, regardless of their age. They may feel responsible for the illness in some way. Did they do something to make their brother or sister sick? Or, they may worry that they will catch the illness.

Adding to their confusion, information may be withheld from them because they are thought to be "too young to understand." Yet children of all ages pick up cues from other family members, which they may misinterpret.

Children may try to overcompensate for ill siblings and attempt to please the parents by becoming "superkids" who never have a problem. At the other extreme, they may start to misbehave at home or at school. They may be teased by other children because their brother or sister is not "normal." They may feel angry at their sick sibling for getting so much attention, and then feel guilty for having such unacceptable feelings, with resulting damage to their self-esteem.

The following are some suggestions to help you and your well children cope with a chronically ill sibling:

—Do not try to hide the child's illness from the well siblings. Even a toddler can feel the change or anxiety in the family. Ask your doctor how to give age-appropriate information and do so early in the illness and at regular intervals as you learn more.

—Explore feelings of sadness, anger, guilt, and responsibility as well as fear of contagion and death with the well siblings. Tell them it is okay to feel these things and that you want to hear about them. Ask about these emotions even if they are not apparent and your well children seem "just fine."

—Have regular family educational sessions with your doctor, nurse, or social worker to answer questions and clarify prognosis. Point out any behavioral changes in the "well" child.

—You will feel overwhelmed at times, so recruit support from neighbors, family, and social or religious groups as well as the hospital.

—Build in extra or special time for well siblings so that they do not feel neglected or resentful. Consider appointing for each well sibling a friend or relative as a "guardian angel" who can provide extra attention.

Reading this book with your child could be just the right starting point for discussion and for healing. Children will identify with Laura, the young girl with a sick brother in the story, and will know that their feelings are acknowledged. Sharing this understanding will help reestablish the closeness between you and your child that is so essential to your child's comfort and well-being.

Laura was two years older than Tom. When he was born, she helped her mommy dress and feed him. And *she* pushed his carriage. Most of the time, she was very glad to be his big sister.

As Tom got older, Laura liked to play with him. When she got home from school, they would rake leaves into a big pile, then run and jump in it. A younger brother could be a lot of fun.

One morning, while Laura was at school, Tom was playing with her favorite doll and the arm broke off. When Laura got home and found it, she was mad. She had told him a hundred times not to touch her dolls!

"You're nothing but a big baby!" she yelled. "I wish I didn't have a brother." Sometimes a younger brother could really be a pain.

Laura and Tom played together almost every day after school, but now it seemed they fought over every little thing. It was not as much fun for Laura because Tom was often tired and cranky.

One afternoon, Aunt Ann was waiting for Laura after school.

"Where's Mommy and Tom?" asked Laura.

"Tom is sick and Mommy is at the hospital with him, so I have come to take you home." Aunt Ann gave Laura a hug and they walked home together.

When Mommy got home, it was very late. She told Laura that Tom had to stay in the hospital for tests and that Daddy was there with him.

That night Laura had trouble getting to sleep. She wondered if it was her fault that Tom got sick. She felt bad about yelling at Tom and wishing she didn't have a brother.

The next day, Laura and her parents went to see Tom at the hospital. He was hooked up to tubes that made strange beeping sounds. He was too weak to sit up. Laura was scared. She wondered if Tom was going to die. When her friend Sally's grandpa went to the hospital, he never came home again.

Tom stayed in the hospital a long time. It was getting colder and all the leaves had fallen from the trees. Laura missed having Tom to play with. Mommy and Daddy didn't have much time for her either because they spent so much time at the hospital.

Everyone asked Laura about Tom.

"How's Tom?" asked her teacher and classmates at school.

"Poor little Tommy. How's he doing?" asked Mr. Lee at the grocery store.

"When will Tom be out of the hospital?" asked their neighbor Mrs. Jackson.

Nobody said, "How are you, Laura?" or "How's school, Laura?" When they asked about Tom, Laura wanted to say, "What about me?"

One night at dinner, Laura said, "Daddy, do you want to hear what I did in school today?"

"Not now, Laura, Mommy and I are talking about Tom."

Laura was so upset she wanted to cry. She sat still and stared at her plate. When Mommy asked her to finish her dinner, Laura screamed, "I don't want to!" She banged her fists down so hard her milk spilled all over the table.

Daddy shouted, "Go to your room right now! I will speak to you later."

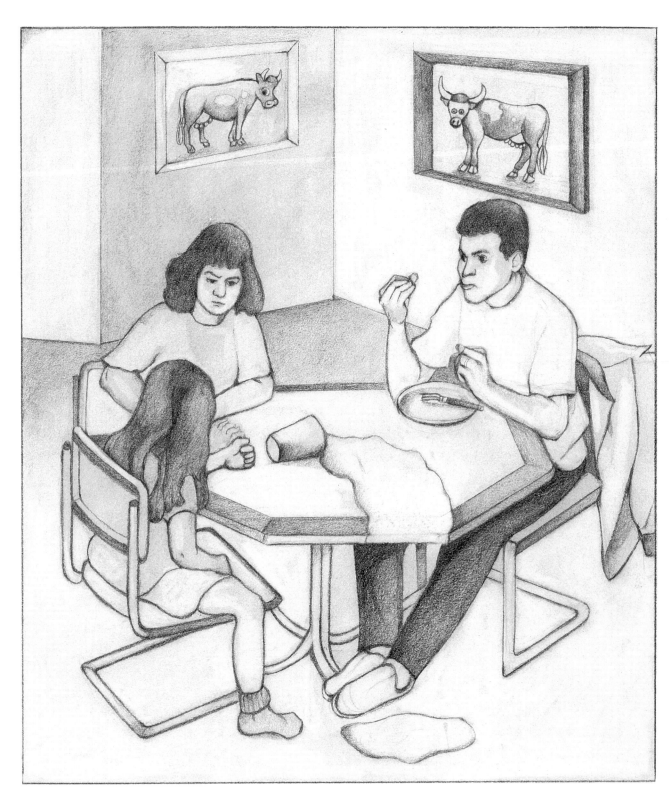

Laura went to her room and waited for Daddy. She was still angry, but she wanted to tell him she was sorry for spilling the milk. But Daddy never came. He had gone to the hospital without saying good night or tucking her in.

The next day, Laura did not want to do anything. She went outside and kicked the last few leaves on the ground. Mommy came out and said, "Laura, come sit on the steps with me."

"I'm sorry if it seems we are ignoring you, honey," said Mommy. "We are very worried about Tom. But Daddy and I love you very much, even if we have not had time to tell you lately."

Laura started to cry. "It's all my fault Tom got sick. That's why Daddy's mad at me. If I hadn't yelled at Tom . . ."

Mommy looked surprised. "Sweetheart, it's not your fault. And Daddy is not mad at you. Nothing you say or think can make someone sick. It is just something that happens. Tomorrow, we will all go to the hospital together to learn more about Tom's illness."

The next day at the hospital, Mommy introduced Laura to Dr. Milson.

"I'm sorry that your brother is sick," said Dr. Milson. She then explained Tom's illness to Laura and her parents. She told them that it was serious but not catching. She said that the medicine seemed to be helping. Tom had to stay in the hospital a little longer, but he would be able to go home soon. He would then have to come back to the hospital once in a while for treatments.

"Can I play with him when he comes home?" asked Laura.

"Yes, indeed," said Dr. Milson. "You can even play with him here as soon as he starts to feel better."

After the meeting, Laura and Mommy and Daddy went to spend time with Tom. He was feeling stronger and gave everyone a hug. Laura sat on Tom's bed, and they started to color together. Laura had learned how to print his name in school and put T - O - M on the top of his picture.

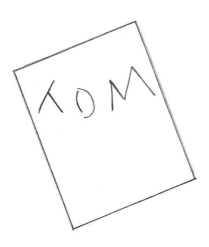

When they left the hospital, Mommy and Daddy took Laura to her favorite restaurant for meatball pizza. Laura told them about one of the hamsters getting loose at school and how everyone, including the teacher, had to walk on tiptoes until he got found! Laura and Mommy and Daddy all laughed together.

Laura ordered her special dessert, a double-dip ice cream cone of vanilla and chocolate with sprinkles. It was Tom's favorite, too.

"When Tom gets home, can we make a special dinner with all the things he likes best?" asked Laura.

"What a great idea," said Daddy. "And you can help make the shopping list, now that you print so well." Daddy gave Laura a big hug.

Then they all held hands and went home together.